Arctic Fox
Polar Bear
frican
wild Dog
Butterfly House
Flamingo
Grey Crowned Crane
Scarlet Ibis
Roseate Spoonbill
hite-faced Saki Monkey
Baboon
Spectacled Langur
Sun Bear
Pygmy Marmoset
Spider monkey
Squirrel Monkey
Tufted Capuchin
Red Panda
Giant Panda
oolly Lemur
Tarsier
Ring-tailed Lemur
Meerkat
Otter
Koala
d Ruffed Lemur
Ring-Tailed Mongoose
Honey Possum
Wallaby
Hyrax
Pine Marten
Possum
Kangaroo
Wombat
Sloth

First pu

The

ww

1 3 5 7 9 10 8 6 4 2

ISBN 978-1-78370-327-2 (hardback)
ISBN 978-1-78370-328-9 (paperback)

This book was typeset in Adobe Garamond Pro, Gill Sans and Adobe Caslon
The illustrations were created with pencil and coloured digitally

Designed by Genevieve Webster
Edited by Katie Haworth

Printed in China

To Catherine
and Mikey

THE MIDNIGHT ZOO
Panda Parade
Jungle Jamboree
Savannah Spectacular
Cat Kingdom

The Jungle Book

She doesn’t believe them, of course.

But we know it’s true.

Mum rushes to meet them.
She hugs them tight and they tell her
everything – all about the flouncing flamingos and
prancing pandas and mischievous monkeys!

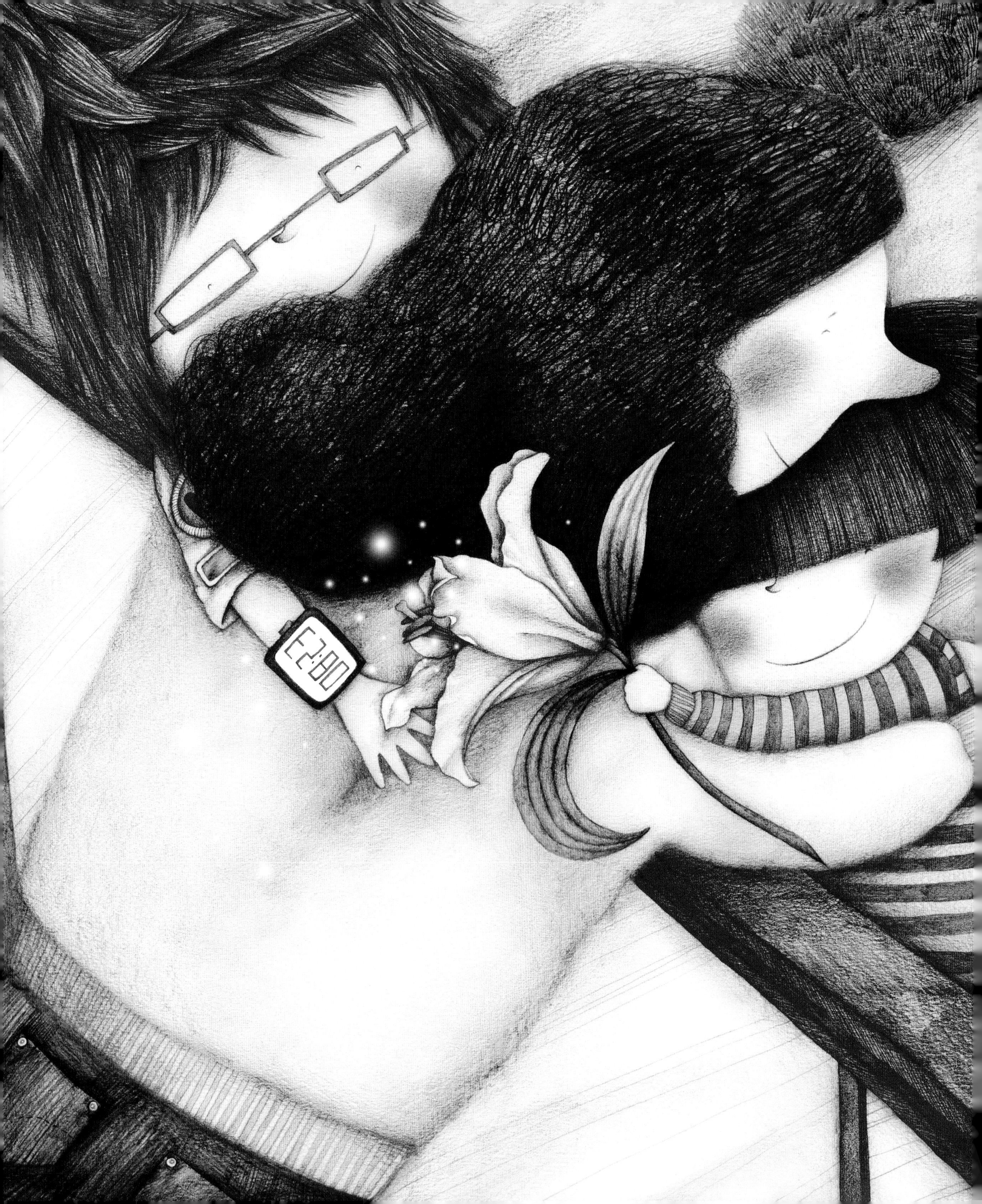

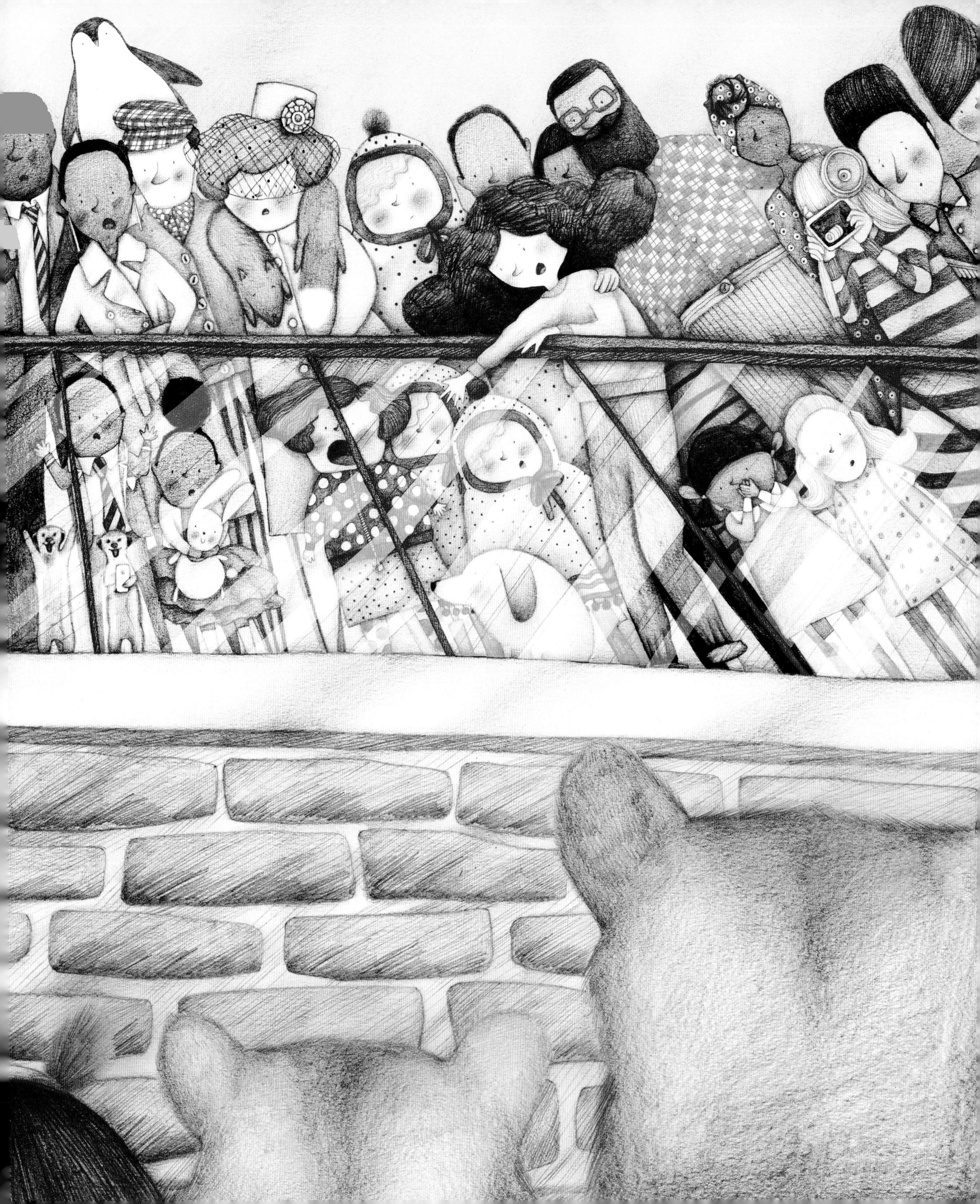

They wake up in the daytime zoo.

. . . and as the sun rises they fall fast asleep.

They see kingly cats in
their comfortable keep . . .

. . . and pandas who prance through
pagodas all night.

Loud, laughing lemurs
with lanterns alight . . .

. . . and mischievous monkeys
in marvellous mountains.

They see flouncing flamingos
and fabulous fountains . . .

. . . they make
a new friend.

And just as the clock strikes midnight . . .

Luckily, Max is very good at being prepared.

Although sometimes Mia has to help him.

LEFT
BEHIND!

For everyone, that is, except Max and Mia,
who suddenly realise they have been . . .

. . . and finally it's time to leave.

NEW NEWS
Mysterious Music coming from zoo at night
THE ZOO
ease up LIFTS
Z
Z
Z
Z

It starts to get late . . .

Cafe

It is very disappointing.

There are no lions.

And not one meerkat . . .

. . . or even a single monkey.

Although Max and Mia do
find some traces of animal life.

But not the flick of a tail or swish of a whisker can be seen.

They have come to see:

lemurs,

flamingos,

red pandas,

and salamanders.

Then they all scamper off around the zoo.
Everyone is so excited!

tickets

And hide at the back like scaredy meerkats.

They nibble like lemurs on some (early) packed lunch.

They trundle like elephants into the car.

And cling like monkeys as Mum says goodbye.

This is Max and Mia, and today is a VERY special day.

Faye Hanson
MIDNIGHT
at
THE
templar publishing